D0933916

World of Reading

These Are the Marvel Super Heroes

© 2015 MARVEL

All rights reserved. Published by Marvel Press, an imprint of Disney Book Group. No part of this book may be reproduced or transmitted in any form or by any means, electronic or mechanical, including photocopying, recording, or by any information storage and retrieval system, without written permission from the publisher.

For information address Marvel Press, 125 West End Avenue, New York, New York 10023.

Printed in the United States of America
First Hardcover Edition, October 2015
3 5 7 9 10 8 6 4 2
FAC-008598-16130
ISBN 978-1-4847-3218-2

For Text Only

This Is Iron Man

Adapted by Clarissa Wong

Illustrated by Andrea Di Vito *and* Rachelle Rosenberg

Based on the Marvel comic book series The Avengers

Los Angeles • New York

© 2015 MARVEL

All rights reserved. Published by Marvel Press, an imprint of Disney Book Group. No part of this book may be reproduced or transmitted in any form or by any means, electronic or mechanical, including photocopying, recording, or by any information storage and retrieval system, without written permission from the publisher. For information address Marvel Press, 125 West End Avenue, New York, New York 10023.

This is Tony Stark.

He owns a company.
It is called Stark Industries.

He makes a lot of money.
Tony is rich.

He has a beach house.

He has an apartment in the city.

Tony has good friends.
He works with his friend
Pepper Potts.

Tony has a friend named
James Rhodes.
Tony calls him Rhodey.
Rhodey works for the army.

Tony has a secret, too.

Tony wears a disk
on his chest.
It keeps him alive.

He made the disk himself.

But that's not all.

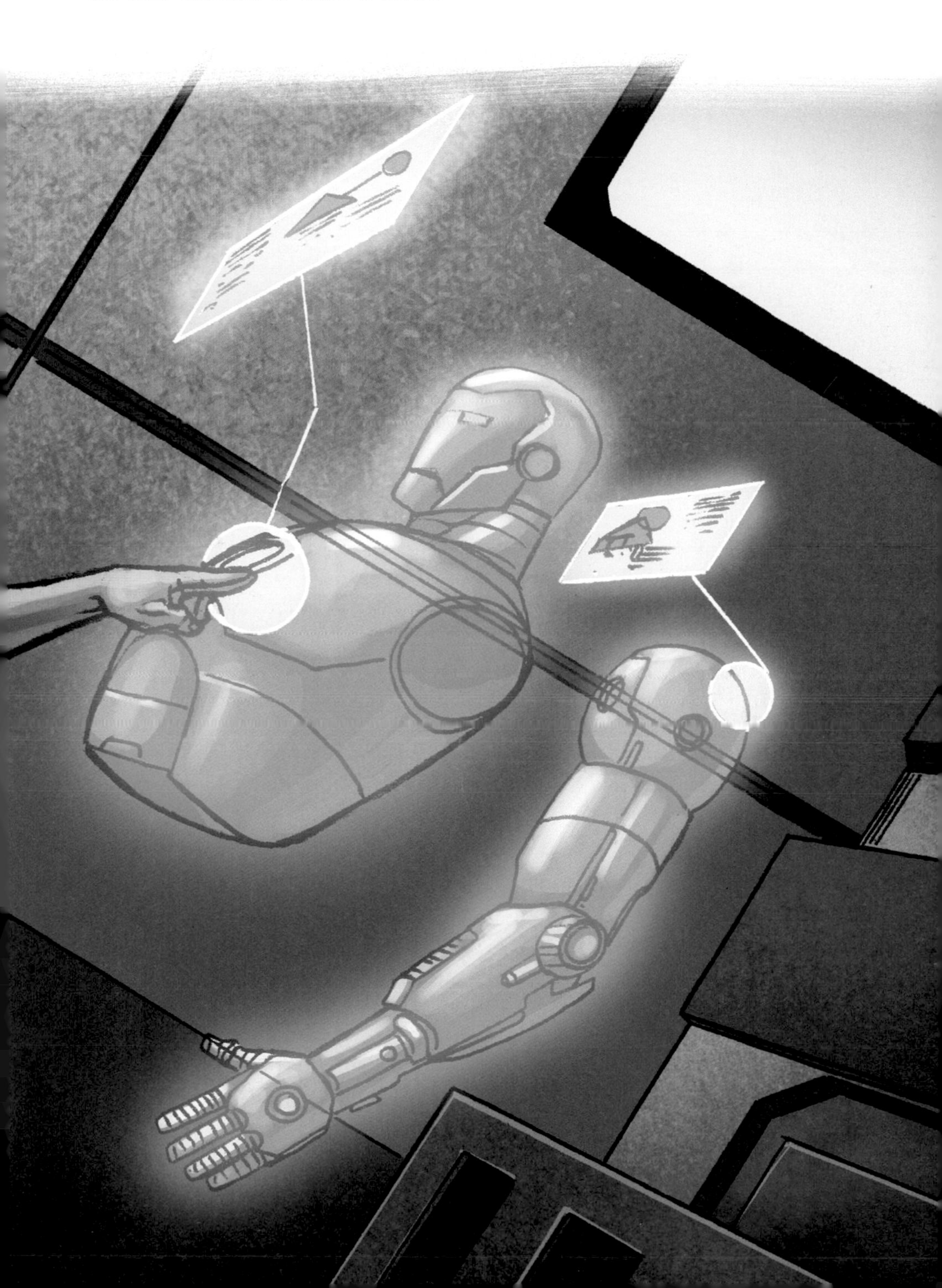

Tony has a bigger secret.
He wears a suit of armor.

He keeps it in a special place.
He works to make it perfect.

Tony puts on the suit.

Then he puts on his helmet.

This is Tony's big secret.
He is a Super Hero!
This is Iron Man!

Iron Man can fly.

He can shoot repulsor blasts.

He fights villains.

Tony's suit of armor
makes him strong.

It makes him powerful.

It makes him a Super Hero!

Tony keeps working
to make his suit better.

He invents new things.

Sometimes they work.

Sometimes they do not work.

But he is always
the invincible Iron Man!

This Is Spider-Man

Adapted by Thomas Macri

Illustrated by Todd Nauck *and* Hi-Fi Design

Based on the Marvel comic book series Spider-Man

Los Angeles • New York

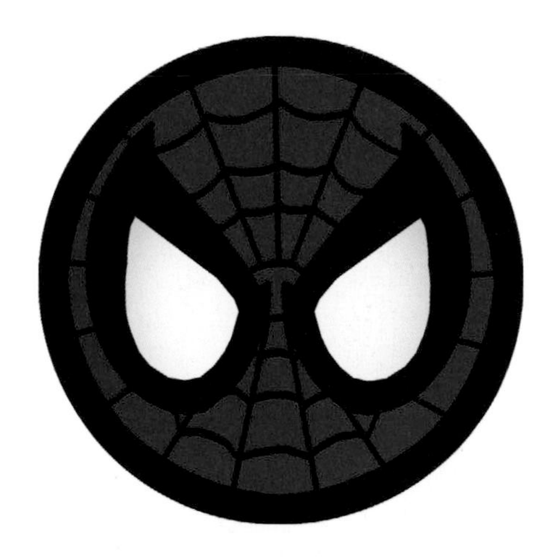

© 2015 MARVEL

All rights reserved. Published by Marvel Press, an imprint of Disney Book Group. No part of this book may be reproduced or transmitted in any form or by any means, electronic or mechanical, including photocopying, recording, or by any information storage and retrieval system, without written permission from the publisher. For information address Marvel Press, 125 West End Avenue, New York, New York 10023.

This is Peter.

Peter lives in Queens.
Queens is in
New York City.

Peter lives with his aunt.
Her name is Aunt May.

Peter loves Aunt May
very much.

Peter is a student.
He goes to high school.

Peter loves school.
He loves math.

He loves science.

Some kids at school are
not nice to Peter.

They push him.
They make fun of him.

Peter does not care.

At home, no one makes fun of Peter.

Peter has a super secret.

He has a costume.

He has web-shooters.

He makes webs.

He shoots webs.

This is his costume.
It has a spider on it.
It has webs on it, too.

Peter puts on his costume.
Peter has a secret name.

He calls himself
Spider-Man.

This is Spider-Man.

Spider-Man can climb
up walls.

He can swing on
his webs.

He shoots his webs.
His webs stop bad guys.

Peter takes off his mask.
He is tired.

Peter goes to sleep.

Peter wakes up. He gets ready for school.

At school, the kids learn
about Spider-Man.

They like Spider-Man.

They do not like Peter.

But they do not know
Peter's secret.

Peter is Spider-Man.

This Is Hulk

Adapted by Chris "Doc" Wyatt

Illustrated by Ron Lim *and* Rachelle Rosenberg

Based on the Marvel comic book series The Avengers

Los Angeles • New York

© 2015 MARVEL

All rights reserved. Published by Marvel Press, an imprint of Disney Book Group. No part of this book may be reproduced or transmitted in any form or by any means, electronic or mechanical, including photocopying, recording, or by any information storage and retrieval system, without written permission from the publisher. For information address Marvel Press, 125 West End Avenue, New York, New York 10023.

This is Hulk.

The Hulk is the strongest!
The Hulk is the biggest!

Hulk gets mad when bad guys try
to hurt good people.
He protects good people.

The madder the Hulk gets,
the stronger he gets.

The Hulk likes to say
“HULK SMASH!”
He is very good
at smashing things.

Hulk looks different
from other heroes.
Some people think
he is a monster.

The Hulk is sad when people treat him like a monster.

Yet the Hulk still protects people.

He even helps the ones
who are mean to him.

The Hulk is not always strong.

Sometimes he is Bruce Banner.
Bruce Banner is a scientist.

One day, before he was the Hulk,
Bruce was testing a bomb.

Oh, no!

Someone walked into the test!

Bruce had to help.

He jumped in.
He saved the boy.
But he got blasted!

The blast turned Bruce into the Hulk!

At first Bruce was scared.
He looked like a monster.

He found out the Hulk
can be good, too.
The Hulk can be a hero!

Whenever Bruce gets very mad,
he grows big and strong.

He turns into the Hulk!

Evildoers should fear the Hulk.

Good people do not have to worry.

An army general
wants to stop the Hulk.

But he will not.

Now the Hulk helps the Avengers.

The Hulk lives in Avengers Tower.

The Hulk and Thor
are best friends.

With the Avengers or alone, the Hulk is always a Super Hero!

These Are the Guardians

Written by Clarissa Wong

Illustrated by Ron Lim *and* Marcelo Pinto

Based on the Marvel comic book series Guardians of the Galaxy

Los Angeles • New York

© 2015 MARVEL

All rights reserved. Published by Marvel Press, an imprint of Disney Book Group. No part of this book may be reproduced or transmitted in any form or by any means, electronic or mechanical, including photocopying, recording, or by any information storage and retrieval system, without written permission from the publisher. For information address Marvel Press, 125 West End Avenue, New York, New York 10023.

These are the
Guardians of the Galaxy.

This is Star-Lord.
He leads the Guardians.
He is a brave leader.

His real name is Peter.
He grew up on Earth.
He loved stars.

His dad was from another world.
Peter wanted to find his dad.
He studied the planets and the stars.

Peter grew up.
He learned to fly.
He became a space pilot.
He was off to the stars!

Peter found his dad.
Peter now lives in space.
Peter learns about different aliens.

There are bad aliens in space.
Peter must protect the stars.
He will find a team to help him.

Peter's father gives him a ship.
He gives him a suit.
The suit gives him powers.

Peter tries on the suit.
Peter becomes Star-Lord!

This is Gamora.
She is a Guardian.

She uses a sword.
She never loses a fight.

This is Drax.
Drax is the strongest.
He has many tattoos.

He looks tough.
He fights tough.

This is Groot.
Groot is big.
He looks like a tree.

© 2015 MARVEL
© 2015 MARVEL
© 2015 MARVEL
© 2015 MARVEL
© 2015 MARVEL
© 2015 MARVEL
© 2015 MARVEL
© 2015 MARVEL
© 2015 MARVEL
© 2015 MARVEL
© 2015 MARVEL
© 2015 MARVEL

© 2015 MARVEL
© 2015 MARVEL
© 2015 MARVEL
© 2015 MARVEL
© 2015 MARVEL
© 2015 MARVEL
© 2015 MARVEL
© 2015 MARVEL
© 2015 MARVEL
© 2015 MARVEL
© 2015 MARVEL
© 2015 MARVEL

He says only one thing.
"I am Groot!"

This is Rocket.
Rocket is tiny.
But he is tough!

Rocket likes to build things.

Some Guardians
are big.
Some Guardians
are small.

Some Guardians
are green.

They follow Star-Lord.
They are a team.

They are the
Guardians of the Galaxy!

They are ready for anything. They use their powers to stop the aliens.

They are strong.
They are brave.

They are ready to fight!
They help one another.
They work together.

Their enemies are strong.
This team is stronger.

They are a powerful group.

The Guardians do not give up.

They take care of each other.
They make a great Super Hero team.

They protect the good.
They protect the planets.
They protect the stars.

They are the Guardians
of the Galaxy!

The New Team

Adapted by Chris "Doc" Wyatt

Illustrated by Andrea Di Vito *and* Rachelle Rosenberg

Based on the Marvel comic book series The Avengers

Los Angeles • New York

© 2015 MARVEL

All rights reserved. Published by Marvel Press, an imprint of Disney Book Group. No part of this book may be reproduced or transmitted in any form or by any means, electronic or mechanical, including photocopying, recording, or by any information storage and retrieval system, without written permission from the publisher. For information address Marvel Press, 125 West End Avenue, New York, New York 10023.

Iron Man and Captain America are Avengers.

Hulk and Thor are also Avengers.

They are all Avengers.
They fight for good.

Sometimes they need help.

That's when they call
the new team of Avengers!

Hawkeye shoots arrows.

He never misses.

Black Widow is a spy.

She fights well in battle, too.

Falcon flies with the wings he built!

He can build new gadgets!

Scarlet Witch has magic.

She can cast spells.

Quicksilver can run fast.

He is faster than
anything on Earth!

Vision is an android.

He can glide through walls.

Some of the new teammates work for S.H.I.E.L.D.

Some can fly.

Some are siblings.

The new team members fight hard.

The new teammates fight for good in the world!

The new team members help their friends!

The Avengers like
their new teammates.

The new team members
like the Avengers.

They are all Avengers!

This Is Ant-Man

Adapted by Chris "Doc" Wyatt

Illustrated by Ron Lim *and* Rachelle Rosenberg

Based on the Marvel comic book character Ant-Man

Los Angeles • New York

© 2015 MARVEL

All rights reserved. Published by Marvel Press, an imprint of Disney Book Group. No part of this book may be reproduced or transmitted in any form or by any means, electronic or mechanical, including photocopying, recording, or by any information storage and retrieval system, without written permission from the publisher. For information address Marvel Press, 125 West End Avenue, New York, New York 10023.

This is Scott Lang.

Scott is Ant-Man.
Ant-Man is a Super Hero!

Scott was not always Ant-Man.
He was once a thief.

Scott stole to support his family.

Scott wanted to teach his daughter
right from wrong.
He decided to stop stealing.
He went back to school to study science.

One day, Scott met a scientist
named Hank.
They talked about science.

Hank gave Scott a special suit.
Scott tried it on.

Scott shrank to the size of an ant!
It was fun at first.

But then ants chased Scott!

Scott got big again
and saved himself!

Soon Scott found a way
to talk to ants.

Then they were his friends.

Scott became Ant-Man.

Ant-Man fights Super Villains.

Ant-Man uses the ants as an army.

Now Ant-Man helps the Avengers.

Being small helps Ant-Man do special things.

Bad guys cannot see him coming.

Ant-Man can fit in small places.

Ant-Man can surprise bad guys!

Ant-Man likes working with Iron Man.

Ant-Man and Iron Man
make a good team.

Ant-Man is very strong!

Ant-Man can turn from big to tiny.

Ant-Man fights for good.

Ant-Man has lots of
Super Hero friends.

They help each other
fight the bad guys!

Ant-Man is a true hero.